WEREWOLVES

A Journal of Transformation

Alice Carr

D1294743

CHRONICLE BOOKS

SAN FRANCISCO

Copyright © 2010 by becker&mayer!

All rights reserved. No part of this book may be reproduced in any form without written permission from the publisher.

Library of Congress Cataloging-in-Publication data is available.

ISBN 978-0-8118-7707-7

WEREWOLVES was produced by becker&mayer!, Bellevue, Washington.

www.beckermayer.com

WEREWOLVES was illustrated by Allyson Haller and written by Paul Jessup.

Design: Kasey Free and Katie Stahnke

Editing: Steve Mockus

Editorial Coordination: Amy Wideman

Production Coordination: Leah Finger

10 9 8 7 6 5 4 3 2 1

Manufactured in China

Chronicle Books LLC

680 Second Street

San Francisco, CA 94107

www.chroniclebooks.com

Saturday, April 12th

Mark and I were attacked by a pack of wild dogs when we were walking through the woods after leaving Katie's party. They were huge — like wolves? There were maybe six of them and they surrounded us. We both got bitten. They knocked us down but I managed to get up and hit one of them hard on the side of the head with a branch. We kept swinging branches and they finally just ran off into the woods, all at once as a group.

It was late but the moon was out, and we've cut through there a million times before. I don't understand where they came from — I didn't think there _were_ any wolves around here.

Their eyes were shiny, like camera red-eye, but without the flash.

I don't know if we should be worried about the bites. They didn't seem RABID, but how can you tell? They weren't foaming at the mouth and they didn't seem sick at all. And the bites aren't very deep — they've already stopped bleeding. WebMD says the first signs of rabies basically show up in a couple months, but then if you have symptoms, you die.

God, my heartbeat is going like crazy. I can't calm down. The party was whatever. My brother is such a _social_ misfit. He's always acting weird, like you can tell he wants to talk to people, but he's always kind of off. I don't know what to do. I bring him to these things and he doesn't really even try. Sometimes I wonder why I do it at all. Going to take a hot shower and try to settle down, and clean out these bites.

Checked on MARK and he's sound asleep.

Sunday,
April 13th

I slept for 13 hours last night. It's already 4pm. I remember mom knocking and coming in to check on me a few hours ago. My muscles hurt. I think that's more from fighting the wolves rather than my potential rabies. The bites don't look all that bad actually.

Had a veggie burger and kind of zoned out in front of the TV. Mark's up but he's still in his room. It's weird, are we going to talk about the attack last night or not? I have some homework I should be doing for tomorrow but really don't feel like it. Kind of spaced out. Usually when I'm spaced out I feel like drawing. I keep thinking about the woods. I grew up around here and the woods never spooked me, but when I mute the TV I can hear sounds — wind blowing and things walking around outside

Monday, April 14th
Study hall

When I got to school I noticed this weird smell in the hallway.
It smelled like blood or pennies, metallic and sweet, like I
could taste it on my tongue. I couldn't really tell where it was
coming from, it was sort of from everywhere. I walked past
these sketchy guys I never talk to, like the kind of guys who
might as well live the rest of their lame lives out smoking
in the parking lot and listening to bad metal. One of them was
kind of beat up looking and as I passed by him and his buddies
HE SMELLED ME.
He actually <u>sniffed</u> me, and then they laughed and kept walking.
So creepy.

HOME

Mark hasn't come home yet. I saw him this morning when I got up. He's supposed to be looking for a job. Maybe that's why he's been out. Talked to Samantha at lunch and she thinks I should go get tested for rabies. She says if they weren't wolves they were dogs, and a pack of dogs is probably feral. I don't know, the bites look better even today.

It was really hard to concentrate at school. Everything seemed sharper? I'm in class every day and it's the same, you know you're just in class, but today it was hard to ignore that everyone's sitting around me, and like someone's fidgeting or tapping their pencil or whatever.

Mark's finally back. Hi, Mark! Mumble mumble. Where were you? Mumble, "Out." Any luck finding a job today? Of course he didn't, right? What kind of job do you look for sulking around wearing a hoodie and never brushing your hair?

Tuesday, April 15th

I called and made an appointment to see the doctor and they said sure come in right away, but on the way there after school I just DIDN'T want to go. DID NOT. Could not. It was this really strong feeling, like something bad would happen to me if I went to the doctor.

Totally irrational and kind of scary.

I kept driving past the clinic and just kept going
and like usual when you just go out driving, you end up at the mall.
My brother was there standing around with those dirtbags from school.
Just like hanging out. So MARK has friends now, and it's these guys?

They all kind of stank, a weird musky smell, like mud or stinkweed. That guy with
the bruise looked like it was almost gone. I wondered if he put a pork chop on it,
like in a cartoon. Too weird for MARK to be hanging out, it felt like I caught
him at something and I felt embarrassed, almost turned around but he called
me over.

"Hey sis."
"Um, hey Bro. What's up?"

"Sis?" What is this, his new cool talk?

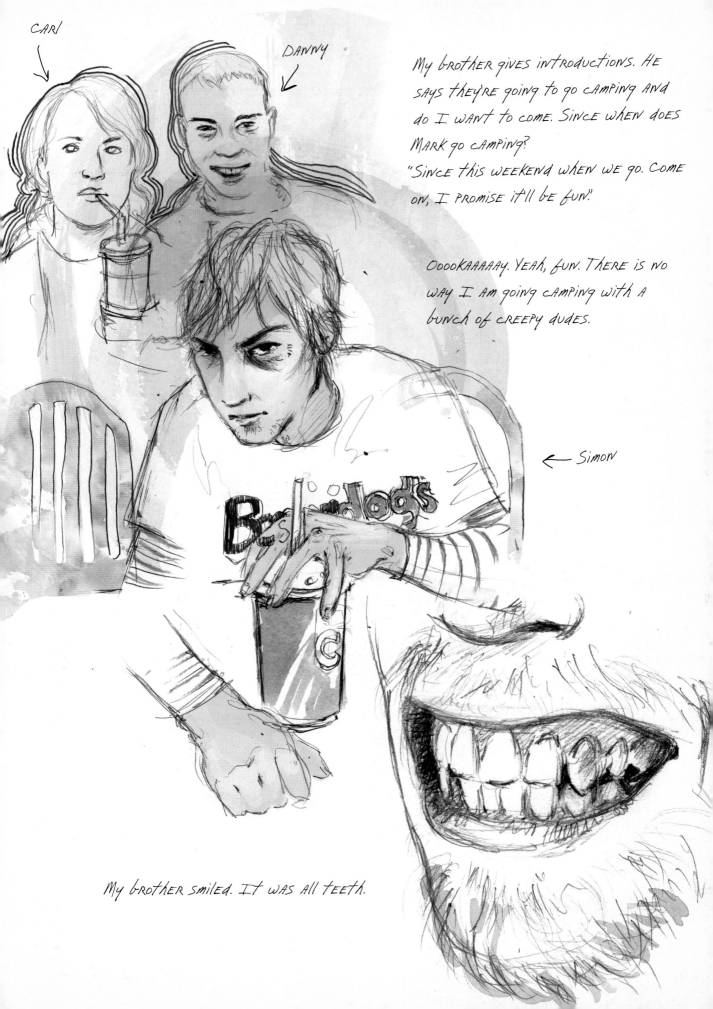

CARL

DANNY

My brother gives introductions. He says they're going to go camping and do I want to come. Since when does Mark go camping?
"Since this weekend when we go. Come on, I promise it'll be fun."

Ooookaaaaay. Yeah, fun. There is no way I am going camping with a bunch of creepy dudes.

← Simon

My brother smiled. It was all teeth.

Checked my bites before going to bed and they're almost totally healed. I think I might call Samantha a little later. Not sure though. I'm tired and just want to go to sleep, but ~~[scribbled out]~~ I'm totally exhausted but also RESTLESS, kind of amped.

CALLED SAMANTHA. SHE'S WORKING ON A PAPER.
SHE'S DISAPPOINTED I DIDN'T GO TO THE
doctor but KNOWS BETTER THAN TO NAG
ME OR I'LL TOTALLY JUST DO THE OPPOSITE ANYWAY.
I told her about the camping invite
and laughed and then she's like,
YOU'RE NOT GOING ARE YOU?

Wednesday,
April 16th

Woke up in the middle of the night with my heart racing and my whole body tense, wide awake and starving. I went down to the kitchen and opened the fridge and found this tray of raw steaks thawing on the top shelf and ~~no one was there.~~ I tore open the plastic and just started gnawing at them. Oh my god was it GOOD. First meat I've had in like three years. I'm standing there and there's meat juice on my face, on the floor, and I didn't care.

I felt more satisfied after eating than I probably ever have.

I licked the tray and licked the little pool of juice off the floor.

I'm just glad no one came in and caught me doing it.

How am I going to explain to my mom where the steaks went?

Thursday, April 17th

Last night I dreamt I was running in the woods, and there were all these rabbits everywhere. Hundreds of them, all running away from me. And I ran after them. Chasing them, tearing them apart. Dream ended with me sitting in a field wearing a necklace of rabbit bones around my neck.

I woke up shaking and hungry and went downstairs and ate a package of lunchmeat while standing in front of the fridge. Replaced the steaks today, going to have to replace the lunchmeat tomorrow. I'm wondering if I should buy some more anyway in case I end up having another of these "midnight snacks."

At school today everybody seemed different.
I don't know, like kind of — rabbity. I wanted to chase them.
Felt kind of lightheaded all day.

Got a text from my brother saying can I meet him in an hour,
he says he has someone he wants me to meet. So that's weird,
but it sounds serious in that way my brother can
get and always means it, whenever he gets serious
about something. Everything feels weird anyway, so OK,
let's just keep going with it.

Mark and his new BFFs pulled up in a station wagon that might as well be held together by duct tape. Not confidence inspiring. Mark says "Hey" and after that no one says anything and we just listen to Ozzy the whole way on the drive out to the woods near the lake. Mark was there and all, but I kept thinking I was glad I brought my mace with me.

I'm not a Teen Girl Goes Missing.

The cabin was near the lake but really well tucked away in the woods off a dirt road. Seemed like the nearest other cabin was probably a long way off. The place was dirty, smelled like mildew and mushrooms and like the firewood stacked on the porch. Cobwebby and spooky I guess if you're never around these sorts of places, but around here that's kind of the norm — everything's dark and dank and left alone. It felt like I'd been there before, even though I hadn't.

I'm supposed to meet someone inside?

Yeah, Mark says, Tomas wants to talk to you.

HE WAS SITTING BY THE FIREPLACE, WHICH WAS EMPTY,
WEARING DIRTY OLD JEANS AND A BEAT-UP COWBOY HAT.
VERY CALM. "HELLO, ALICE."

Hi.

"I'M SURE YOU HAVE A LOT OF QUESTIONS. BUT FIRST, LET ME
EXPLAIN SOME THINGS TO YOU. SIT, PLEASE." AND THEN THE GUYS
ALL WENT OUT TO THE PORCH. I DIDN'T LIKE THAT. IT FELT
LIKE I'D BEEN DELIVERED OR SOMETHING, BUT THEY DIDN'T
SEEM TO BE GOING ANYWHERE, JUST OUTSIDE SMOKING. I KEPT
AN EYE ON THE CAR BUT NO ONE WAS HEADING TOWARD IT.
MARK WOULD NEVER PUT ME IN DANGER. WHOEVER THIS GUY WAS,
MARK TRUSTED HIM.

I REMEMBER HIS WORDS REALLY CLEARLY. ESPECIALLY IF I CLOSE MY EYES.

"YOU'VE PROBABLY NOTICED SOME CHANGES OVER THE LAST FEW DAYS, JUST AS YOUR
BROTHER HAS. YOU AND YOUR BROTHER WERE WELCOMED INTO OUR PACK, OUR FAMILY,
WHEN WE FOUND YOU IN THE WOODS. THE BITES WE GAVE YOU BOTH, WHICH BY NOW
WILL HAVE HEALED, WERE YOUR INITIATION. THEY'RE YOUR FIRST STEP INTO A NEW
LIFE, BUT ALSO A VERY OLD WAY OF LIFE, RULED BY ANIMAL NATURE AND THE CYCLES
OF THE MOON. THE YOUNG MEN WHO I CAN SEE YOU WONDER ABOUT ARE
ALSO RECENTLY WELCOMED, BUT WITH SEVERAL CYCLES BEHIND THEM ALREADY.
I HAVE SEEN MANY CYCLES. THE LONGER YOU LIVE WITH THE ANIMAL NATURE, THE
BETTER YOU WILL BE ABLE TO UNDERSTAND AND CONTROL THE IMPULSES. YOU, AND
YOUR BROTHER, AND THESE OTHER BOYS TO DIFFERENT EXTENTS, ARE ALL LEARNING
WHO AND WHAT YOU ARE NOW.
YOU ARE HUMANS, BUT YOU ARE NOW ALSO WOLVES."

The boys were fighting on the porch. Wrestling? And I couldn't tell at first if they were playing around. I looked at Tomas and he seemed unconcerned, and that made me feel calm.

"I can help you and your brother learn more about your nature, just as I am teaching these boys. The pack offers community, but it also offers protection. There are those who misunderstand us. Most do. We can manage this by secluding ourselves when the light of the moon shines most brightly. There are also those who hunt us. For this reason we band together, keeping each other safe from harm. Those who seek to destroy us consider who we are — human and animal at once — an abomination. As though nature could offend itself. Let us protect you, and let me show you how to control your wolf-self and discover your true power. There is much to learn. Your brother has already joined us."

I didn't get it yet. "Do I look like I want to join some sort of new age wolf cult? I love Mark, but he'd 'join' anything or anyone that would have him. Is he giving you money? Is that what you want?"

Tomas stood up from his chair and looked at me. Then he closed his eyes and bent suddenly, like his insides constricted, and then his bones started to — move. It couldn't have happened, but it did happen. I watched it happen.

His face pushed outward. His hands pulled in for a second, like when you burn yourself on an iron, and then they moved outward, larger. His knees bent slightly backward and his back made a popping sound. There was new hair on his face and hands. He opened his eyes, yellow, and froze what was happening in place, looking at me for a moment and breathing hard before his body pulled back into itself. He sat back down in the chair. All the boys on the porch were looking in through the windows now. I felt sick.

I've been up all night writing and drawing since
they dropped me off at home and it's calming me down.
It's almost morning.
Mark went back with them to the cabin. At least
that's what they said they were going to do. Since
I got home I keep hearing twigs snapping, branches
from the trees outside (?) scraping the house in the
wind. There's also a strong, musky smell, what I'm
starting to understand as a wolf smell.

Are they outside? Waiting for me? Watching me?
I don't know. I need to sleep.

Friday, April 18th

Two hours sleep. School's a total blur. I don't know
what to think about last night, and being super tired
isn't helping me think straight. It feels like a dream
but I know that it wasn't. How could it not be though?

I just went out for a walk and it felt good to be outside but I think
this van started following me. Black van, with the windows tinted.
At first I thought it might be Tomas and my brother's friends, but
it didn't feel like them somehow. I could tell I was being followed
without even seeing the van at first. It was just like the saying,
all the hair stood up on the back of my neck and then I turned
around and there it was. I was mad. I took a couple steps toward it
before I stopped myself. What, am I going to run up and
~~attack~~ attack it? I thought maybe I shouldn't go home cause
they'll know where I live, but I figured that whoever they are they
must already know that, so I just went home.

Mom's wondering about Mark. He's been away more than usual even. I told her that he was hanging around with this new crew and that seemed to satisfy her somewhat, but I left a lot out. Tomas. The van. She's making pasta and usually makes two sauces, veggie for me and meat for her and Mark, when he's around. I tell her that she should just make the meat and I'll eat it and she's happy, like "Honey that's wonderful! I was so worried you weren't getting enough protein when you were going through that phase." I confess to the lunchmeat snack — I can't tell her I ate raw steaks — and she says, well, if you were craving it like that then your body must have really needed it and you should listen to that.

I just looked up what phase the moon is going to be tonight. Tonight is Waxing Gibbous. Means I have a few days and then it'll be the full moon. What will happen then? Will I turn into a wolf? Can I turn into one now? I need to know more. Will do some research online and go to the library tomorrow.

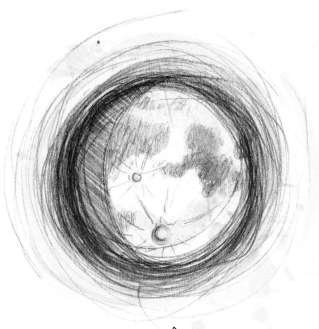

waxing gibbous moon

Saturday,
April 19th

Sam's here. Hi Sam!

Went jogging. Felt <u>really</u> good, better than usual. Sam says I seem different, not just the bugging out with the meat or the stuff with my brother's weird friends, but like physically different. Burly. It was hard to keep pace with her, I kept wanting to just take off, and usually she's the one pushing. I told her about the van, and whatever she thinks about all the wolf stuff — I think she's probably humoring me, I mean what would you think? — she's sure about the van, and it's scary. She made me promise not to go out jogging alone. I said yes but god I want to go out jogging again RIGHT NOW, even though we just got back. The Tomas stuff, that's hard to understand. And really if I hadn't seen him change? What would I believe, what do I believe? What did I really see?

WE grabbed burritos for lunch. Sam's usual tofu, me carne asada, which she thinks is gross. "Is this a phase or are you one of them now?" She means carnivores, "the enemy" when we both went veggie.

But I get it. I mean really, I think if you understand where the meat comes from and don't pretend it comes from nowhere, you have every right to eat it. It doesn't come from nowhere, it comes from animals. Even animals eat other animals.

Well, the internet is a wealth of information you don't know how to trust. "Real" pictures of "werewolves" screengrabbed from movies, or photoshop disasters, or just who knows where this stuff came from.

A lot of the "facts" seem to come from books and movies, and I've seen these movies too, and so what? So that makes it true? Then there are these Lycanthrope Forums where nerd shut-ins fantasize about their "wolf lives."

The Werewolf: Lost in the Dark Forum

http://forum.werewolf.viewtopic.php?id=435

werewolf forum

News (372) ▾ Popular ▾

http://... werewo... http://i... Studio ... http://i... http://i... werew... werew... The We... Charac... underw... werew...

From: The Boulevard of Broken Dreams

Offline

5-01 23:49:38

Shadowfang
New Moon ELder

From: The Desert West of the Rockies

Website

Offline

#14

I CANNOT CONTROL MY CRAVINGS ANY LONGER. I USED TO FIGHT THE HUNGER INSIDE ME, BUT I KNOW IT'S HOPELESS AND WHY FIGHT AGAINST IT. I GROW STRONGER WITH THE MOON, AND IF THEY KNEW MY POWER THEY WOULD FEAR ME

-02 00:10:38

Fenris Malquoi The White
Half Moon Hunter

#15

yo, I'm Fenris Malquoi The White, but thats a mouthful so everyone call me fenris

Ooookay. The older stuff seems more believable, but is that just because it's older and fits with the stories in the movies, the old and legendary parts? Accounts of wolves in the forest of Europe for centuries and legends of man-wolves infected and terrorizing villages until they're killed by silver weapons. Pretty much everyone seems to think that being a werewolf is a "curse," and it always seems to end up with the werewolf getting killed by humans. I don't like that. No one ever talks about there being a cure. I don't see anything about werewolves getting old.

   Seems like they don't really get the chance.

Back from the library. I don't know why seeing something in a book feels more trustworthy than reading it on the internet. It feels more physical, like the books are bricks and you can stack them up and it feels real, but I don't know, the library's basically just a less efficient paper internet. The stuff on werewolves is shelved in folklore, which is sort of already admitting that it's all probably made up, but anyway. Everyone agrees that if you get bitten by a werewolf, you become a werewolf. So if Tomas is right and if they're werewolves, then so are me and Mark.

Went for a jog, or a run. Ran as fast as I wanted to.

Tomorrow's the full moon.

Sunday, April 20th

I slept in too long. Didn't wake up until almost 3pm.
Today is supposed to be the first night of the full moon, and I don't
know if it's power of suggestion or it's just that achy feeling you get if
you sleep in way too long but I think I can feel it in my muscles and
maybe even my bones. Splitting time today working on my English paper
and reading the werewolf forum. There's a lot of talk about werewolf
"hunters," who sound scary if any of this is true. Apparently they trace
their hunting back to the way that werewolves supposedly used to be
driven out of villages and hunted and killed centuries ago, so it's like
some time-honored vocation. They also used to double as "witch-finders."
That's scary right there. If someone just thought you were a witch,
they'd just burn you or drown you. So whether you actually are a
werewolf or not, if they even just THINK you are, you're in trouble.
Assuming this isn't all some sort of Civil War reenactor's role-playing
stuff and everyone on here isn't just playing along, which is totally
possible, I mean ... World of WARCRAFT? Hello?

Mark texted.

    MARK FULL MOON TNT. SAFER W US.
        COME 2 CABIN, I COME GET U?

    ME R U HIGH?

    MARK NT KIDDING

    ME IM OK

    MARK DON'T THINK SO

Monday, April 21st

I woke up just before dawn this morning lying next to a creek.
My clothes were shredded. There were leaves matted in my hair
and a rabbit carcass next to me. My mouth tasted like I licked
the end of a battery. My hands were bloody and I could see when
I got home and looked in the mirror so was my mouth. I'm so lucky
it was still dark. It was hard to figure out where I was but I
wandered till I saw the cell tower and knew where I was, not too
far from home, in the woods.

I remember going for a run last night, really needing to get outside
and MOVE, especially after the sun went down. The air was cold on
my arms and felt good. I didn't see the van for almost an hour and
then I turned a corner and there it was, parked and waiting.
The side door started to slide open and it was like my whole body like
every cell jumped all at once and I RAN. I remember sounds and
smells and textures in the woods but from up close, not from a human
height, lower to the ground. My muscles HURT. Worse than any time
after doing some new sport and discovering muscles you didn't know
you had. Agony. But it also kind of feels good. I don't feel PARALYZED
like after we went cross-country skiing and I couldn't walk down
the stairs the next day. I feel — flexible, maybe what it feels like
if you're double-jointed.

The blood had to have been from the rabbit? So I ate
a rabbit last night? I've graduated from steaks in
the kitchen. Washed off the blood in the shower after
doing the drawing and got clothes from the hamper
and am in bed now before Mom wakes up.
Of course MARK hasn't been here for days.

Blew off school. Had Mom call me in sick.

That was easy. She felt my head and said I was burning up.

I woke up feeling all keyed up, like my whole body is tense, like a spring. Jumpy.

My senses seem overloaded, everything's super-intense.

It's late and there's a message from Mark asking <u>Am I okay? Where am I?</u> which he left last night. I didn't have my phone with me when I was running. I call Mark back. He was at the cabin and out "camping" with the other guys and Tomas. I tell him about the van, and the rabbit. He says I have to come to the cabin now, before it gets dark, because the changes will happen again tonight and it won't be safe if the men in the van know where I am. How am I supposed to get there? Go out the back door and cut through the woods and get Sam to pick you up and take you he says.

Sam came and picked me up. I took a bag of stuff with me.
Left a note for Mom. "CAMPING" seems to be the best excuse.
I told Sam about the rabbit and she didn't really know what
to say. Pretty much are you OK and what can I do to help?
But I can tell she's talking to me like you might talk to someone
a little crazy, but you're not calling them on the crazy parts
cause that'll make them not want your help, so you end up making
tinfoil hats with them to ward off the Martians while you try to
figure out a better way to help.

Sam dropped me at the cabin, which looks and smells pretty much exactly like a bunch of boys are living in it.

Here is the amazing squalor.

TOMAS AND I TALKED ABOUT WHAT'S HAPPENED. HE'S SAYS HE'S GLAD I'M HERE
  THOUGH HE ASKED ABOUT HOW I GOT HERE AND SEEMS MOSTLY SATISFIED
  WE WEREN'T FOLLOWED.
HE ASKED WHAT I TOLD SAM AND I SAY I DON'T REALLY <u>KNOW</u>
WHAT'S GOING ON ENOUGH TO TELL SAM ANYTHING.

  THE VAN BELONGS TO THE HUNTERS. APPARENTLY THE BEST TIME FOR THEM
  TO COME AFTER US IS CLOSE TO THE FULL MOON WHEN IT'S HARD FOR US
  TO CONTROL OUR CHANGES, BUT NOT ON THE FULL MOON, WHEN WE'RE
  STRONGEST. THEY HAVE SOME KIND OF CODE WHERE THEY'RE ONLY SUPPOSED
  TO DISPATCH US WHEN IN WOLF FORM, TO BE SURE WHAT WE ARE.

  I ASK: "DISPATCH?"

  TOMAS: "KILL."

  THEY USE WEAPONS THAT ARE MADE OF SILVER,
  WHICH IS TOXIC AND MAKES WOUNDS THAT ARE HARD
  TO HEAL, AND WOLFSBANE, WHICH IS REALLY NASTY.

Tuesday, April 22nd

Tomas says the pack hunts together almost every night. We don't need the full moon to change, it just makes it easier, less painful, and it's also less painful with experience.

We hunted last night. It HURT. My bones felt too big and stretched under my skin and my hair bristled and everything was moving, it felt like everything was sprained or breaking and healing all at the same time, like I got hit by a truck and healed up in a different shape. I could see the same thing happening to the boys.

Sensations in the forest were overwhelming and sharp, smells and shapes and things were a blur but I could also tell what they were and how they were supposed to be, even if they weren't totally in focus as we were running. We ran and I have never felt so free running ~~as~~ as a human — that is such a weird thing to write or even think.

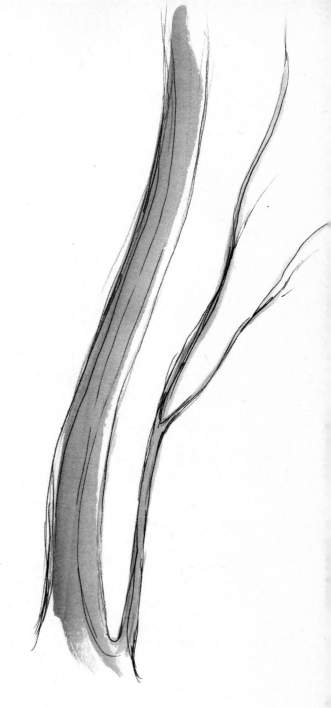

We didn't catch anything but I could tell what was out there, deer and rabbits and other animals. I could smell streams and could even smell what felt like safe smells, which Tomas explained as the smell of dens, either that he had prepared or that were naturally going to be of use for us on nights when we don't return to the cabin.

EVERYONE'S completely wired today After last night.
Tonight's another hunt and the boys have been acting like
~~[scribbled out]~~ animals.

They keep picking on my brother.
Shoving him. Snapping their teeth in his face.
I hate it, but he's not fighting back, he's just sort of rolling over.
He's acting like he's playing along, but he's not,
and what they're doing doesn't feel like playing.

Wednesday,
April 23rd

We made a kill. It was ~~good~~ fantastic. A beautiful deer.
We tracked it, surrounded it, attacked it, ate it. We tore it
open and ate it down to the bones. I still remember the taste
of its blood and meat in my mouth.

We woke up after the hunt in a den that Tomas had prepared for us. Everyone was naked. It didn't feel weird at the time, but it feels weird now after the fact when I'm writing this. There was a stash of clothes and some water and stuff to clean up with. We all woke up super thirsty. The hunt and the kill didn't feel weird at the time either, it felt soooo good, but now today I feel a little queasy.

Is that because I am uncomfortable that I ate a live deer, or is it just hard to digest?

Kills aren't that common, Tomas says, and the boys hadn't even had one yet, that was the first.
We went out again last night and I made a point of watching myself change in the mirror.

Me, from memory.

Thursday, April 24th

Mom must be FREAKING OUT. It's been four days. I called and left a message saying I was still on the trip and I'd be back soon, that it was part of a school program. I don't know if she'll buy that but I don't know what else to do. Texted Sam and said I'm OK, talk soon. Does anyone else wonder where I am? What are we supposed to do about going back to normal life? Is that even possible anymore? I'm starting to freak out.

I talked to my brother alone and he's like, "This is so amazing, I wish this had happened years ago, isn't this great?!"

What about Mom?

"We'll tell her something."

What?

"I don't know."

What about the guys in the van, the hunters who know who we are now?

"They're not going to mess with us."

They're already messing with us, they were following me! What about the other guys beating on you all the time?

"They're just playing around. I don't mind. It'll die down."

COME ON. I tried to look him in the eye when he said this but he wouldn't look at me.

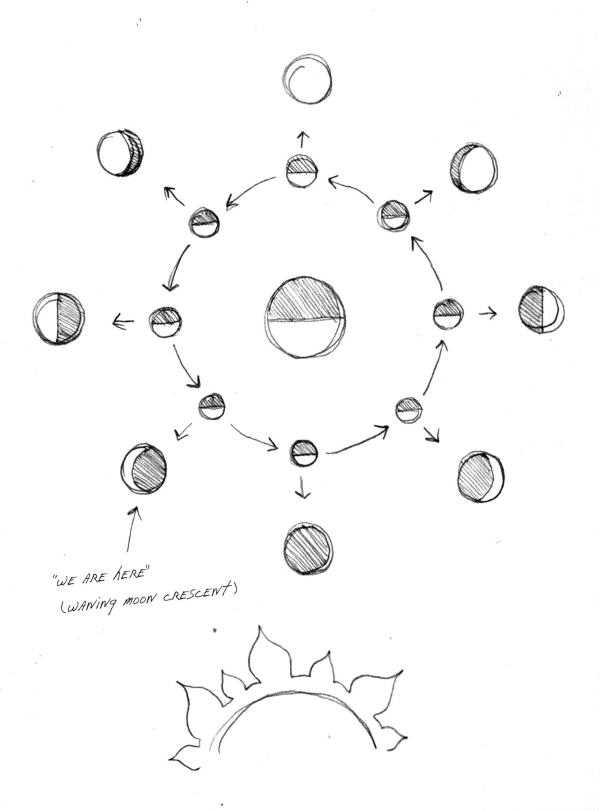

"WE ARE HERE"
(WANING MOON CRESCENT)

Friday, April 25th

Tomas is explaining more about the importance of planning ahead, of the
stashes of clothing — that explains the thrift store look everyone's sporting,
why buy nice clothes if you're just going to shred them — and of the dens
and getting away when we need to be wolves, and how learning to control our
transformations will let us live as much a part of human society as we want to.
So being a wolf is like joining the national guard, "serve just one weekend
a month" kind of thing? What about the hunters? Tomas promises that they'll
leave us alone after we learn to control our impulses and live by the rules.

Who made the rules?

"The rules have been in place for a very long time."

Okay so why are they after Tomas? Won't they still come after us?

"I, well I will just say that I haven't been playing by the rules, so far as
they are concerned. But you will be fine."

US AS WOLVES

Saturday, April 26th

We've been hunting but still no kill.

Last night I dreamed that I was surrounded by animals and I was eating and eating and tearing them apart, but they didn't mind.

was talking to Danny. He and the other guys knew each other before. He said they were out drinking beer in the woods one night when Tomas attacked and bit them, a few weeks before Mark and me. He doesn't seem too concerned about getting back anytime soon. He's _way_ into it, like Mark's into it.
He said he was glad to have us join, that me and Mark coming helped "strengthen the pack."

According to Danny, it works like a real wolf pack. There's the pack but then there are two members that have specific roles, the alpha and the omega. The alpha is dominant and the others follow it as an example of strength. The omega is the lowest and is put in its place by the rest of the pack, and this is like the role it serves. What? I guess to make everyone else feel good about themselves?

The alpha's obviously Tomas, right, and the omega is —
I knew the answer.

"Your brother."

I told MARK what I've found out about the PACK, that basically
he's their whipping boy and PROBABLY always will be, that it's that
WAY ON PURPOSE. It's not going to get any better.

"How do you know?"

DANNY told me.

"Well, what does he know?"

Is he that grateful just to be included? So yeah, being a wolf = POWER,
but this is the absolute worst he's ever been picked on. This is violent.
They don't just SNAP at him, they bite. It heals fast so it's no big deal, right?
MARK doesn't CARE, right? WE've been eating dinner — meat, lots of it —
since we haven't had a kill and so MARK's reaching across the table and
CARL barks and his jaw SNAPS and I totally jump. MARK didn't EVEN
really flinch. DANNY kept his eyes on me the whole time.

Sunday, April 27th

I woke up earlier than everyone else this morning. I'm still mad about the Mark thing. Even if he's okay with it, how can he be, I'm not okay with it. Or that now suddenly we're part of this group we have to stick together with for our own safety, even if I hate them? What if I want my old life back? How much of it can I have back at this point?

I took the keys to Tomas's car and drove into town and parked and just got out and walked around. Streets, shops, traffic, people. They're all still here.

I was heading back to the car when two guys I'd never seen before walked right up to me and said "Hi Alice". Instinct, I crouched, I tensed up, all my arm hair standing up. My ears would have gone back, I could feel the muscles. How did they know who I was?

"We know you and your brother."

They want to talk to me, they say, "Let's go to the diner down the block and get something to eat. Did they think I was stupid?

"It's broad daylight and we're in the middle of town, surrounded by people. Come on, we have a lot to talk about."

OK. Why not.

We sat down in the corner away from everyone. I tried to order the vegetarian omelet and they both laughed at me, "Alice, come on," so I ordered a hamburger. They're hunters, right, so why are they doing this, what are they doing, what do they want from me?

Bob LOOK WE UNDERSTAND THAT THIS ISN'T YOU OR YOUR BROTHER'S FAULT,
OR YOUR DECISION TO GET CAUGHT UP IN THIS.
   DAVE AS FAR AS WE'RE CONCERNED, YOU'RE VICTIMS HERE.
   YOU DIDN'T ASK FOR THIS, AND WE'RE NOT AFTER YOU.

YOU'RE NOT? SO WHY WERE YOU FOLLOWING ME AROUND IN YOUR CREEPY VAN?

DAVE WE'RE NOT INTERESTED IN YOU. WE'RE INTERESTED IN TOMAS. HE'S BEEN DOING THIS
FOR A LONG TIME. HE GOES FROM TOWN TO TOWN AND HE INFECTS —
Bob NO OFFENSE.
DAVE HE INFECTS SOME YOUNG PEOPLE TO SERVE AS A NEW PACK, TO PROTECT HIMSELF —

FROM YOU.

Bob YES, BUT—

SEE THIS IS SCARY. WHY DOES HE NEED PROTECTION FROM YOU?
WHY DON'T I NEED PROTECTION FROM YOU?

   Bob THE PROBLEM HERE IS THAT HE INVOLVES PEOPLE IN THIS AGAINST THEIR WILL, AND
   WORKS THEM UP INTO A STATE OF AGITATION SO THAT THEY DO GET THEMSELVES INVOLVED,
   THEY ENGAGE IN CONFLICT, AND WHEN THAT HAPPENS, SOMETIMES PEOPLE GET HURT, ON
   BOTH SIDES. IT'S RECKLESS, IT'S IRRESPONSIBLE.
   DAVE IF YOU COULD CHOOSE TO DO THIS WHOLE THING ALL OVER AGAIN, WOULD YOU CHOOSE
   THE LIFE YOU HAVE NOW?

   I DON'T TELL THEM THAT MY BROTHER MIGHT.

   Bob LOOK, THINGS ARE THE WAY THEY ARE AT THIS POINT. GO KILL A DEER ONCE A MONTH,
   WHAT DO WE CARE? YOU THINK WE GO SNUFFING EVERY WEREWOLF UP AND DOWN THE
   COUNTRY HERE? THERE'D BE BODIES—
   DAVE BOB—
   Bob OKAY, OKAY.

   THEY PAID FOR THE HAMBURGERS.

Outside I say, I don't think you're telling me everything.

They say, All you need to know is that we will leave you and your brother alone. You can go back to the life you had before. All we want is Tomas.

We trade cell numbers. I say, You're going to follow me.

They say, No we won't. You're parked over there, we're walking this way, see? Call. This is your way out before things get out of hand.

I watched them drive off in the other direction. I circled a few random blocks and even parked for a while to make sure they were gone before heading back to the cabin.

When I got back everyone was ready to pounce. Where was I?
I didn't even try to pretend, I told them I got lonely for
town and that the hunters came, and I told them that they
said they were only after Tomas. The boys, even my brother,
were MAD. Tomas says, you were followed.

No, I was careful.

"No, you were followed. We have to leave at once."

Everyone started packing up immediately. Nobody really has all that
much, but Tomas told us only take what we can carry. As we walked
outside, Tomas headed straight for the woods and the boys followed.
I asked Tomas, aren't we going to take your car? "It's not my car,"
he says. We left it and walked into the woods.

We're headed to a farmhouse that Tomas knows about — one of the benefits of his preparedness deal is that he always has a Plan B in mind. We're all practiced enough with our animal vision that we don't need any light but the moon to make our way. We're traveling as humans rather than wolves — although we'd be able to cover the ground faster that way — because if we wolf out, we'll lose all our stuff.

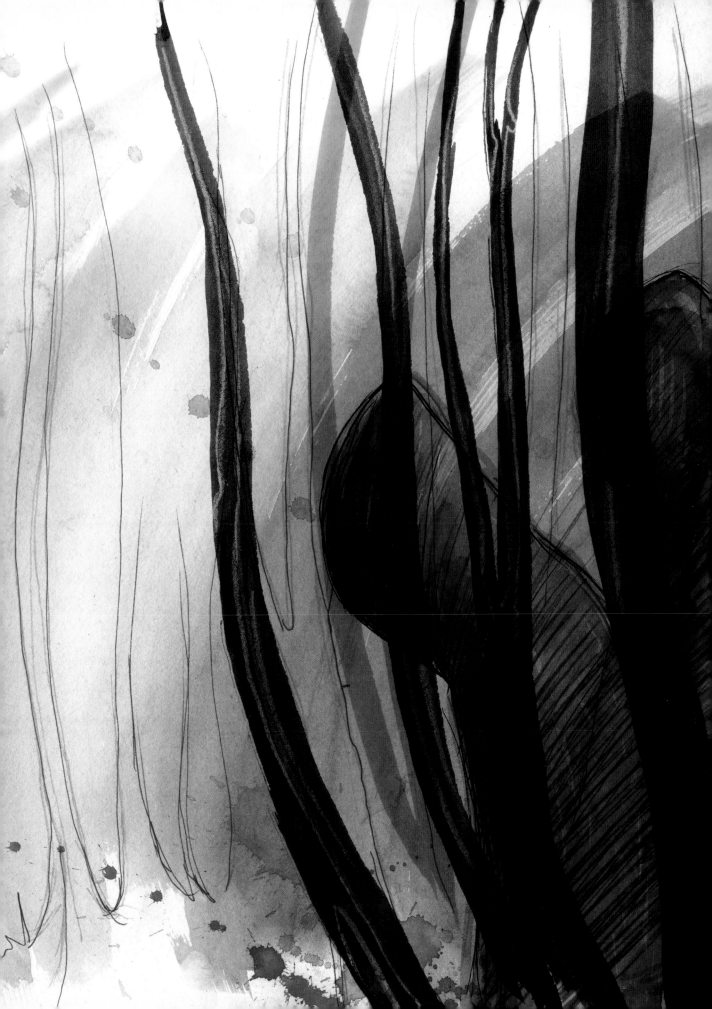

Monday, April 28th

I got a text from Sam today — I kind of jumped when I felt the phone vibrate, I didn't think there'd be any reception out here. She says she's been doing some poking around and there's a researcher at Case Western Reserve who's been studying lycanthropy and DNA and the gist of the article is that it's a scandal that she got some government money to do this obviously crackpot research. I mean, WEREWOLVES, right? Sam's going to look into it some more.

We're going to sleep in the rough tonight, in a clump to share body heat and stay warm, no fire, to keep a low profile. Tomas is semi-transformed and is standing watch, listening and sniffing.

Tuesday, April 29th

We heard some branches breaking last night in the woods not too
far from us and I was up and had transformed partway
but then stopped like on a dime when Tomas motioned to stop —
he wants us to stay human while we're in the open so that we
stay in better control of ourselves, not run off and everything.
I didn't know I had that much control already. Carl and Razor
were up too. Razor sniffed and said "I think it's a deer, let's get it!"
and Tomas said sometimes they bring deer, and if they're good
they know how to mask their scent, though he can usually tell.

We stayed put and didn't hear it again.

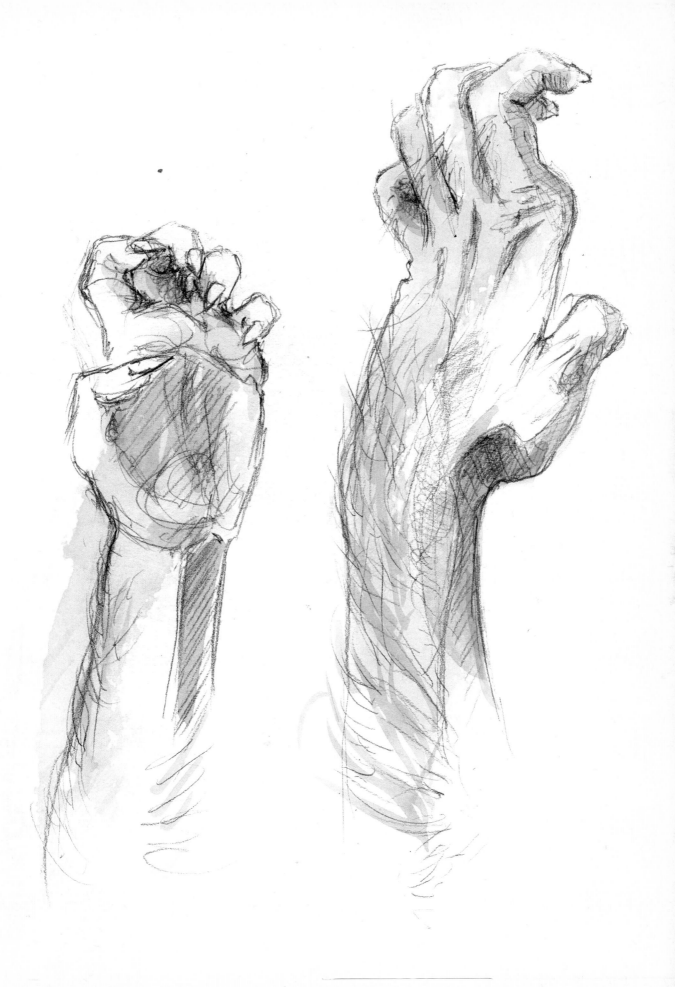

We made it to the farmhouse this afternoon. It's big and kind of boarded up but not like a dump or anything — how does Tomas know about these places? It actually looks really safe, the boarded up situation kind of being a defense if it came to that. It didn't take too long to find a way in and also not too long to shut the opening from inside.

After investigating the place, some abandoned furniture and whatever, we took naps and now are all in front of a fire. Tomas said he thought it was safe to build one. When you're a wolf, the forest is the best. When we had to stay human out there, what I was craving more than anything was to be indoors. Now that we're here and our stuff is squared away, we're itching to go out and roam the forest and hunt. It's been too long keeping the wolves inside.

Maybe it was a bad idea, but I asked Tomas if he knew anything about the RESEARCHER.

"Ah, yes. The cure. But the cure to what? Afflictions are cured. Humans, they can't smell, they can't see, they can't hear, can't feel. Nature is scary for them. We're alive, and this is somehow a threat."

There's a cure?

It's hard to get down here what it feels like to be in the forest. It's like there are three versions of the forest all overlapping — what it smells like, what it looks like, and what it sounds like, and before, I mean when I didn't have these senses the way I do now, I remember being outside at night and if you were walking around and heard something, you would STOP and then strain to see what it was, or to hear it better. Never mind being able to smell it. But now I might smell something first, and I CAN SEE it OR hear it clearly while I'm still in motion, AT A RUN.

Thursday, May 1st

FINALLY, ANOTHER KILL. NOT MUCH, but with two kills now I get it, it's just totally nothing like EATING something we've bought, EVEN if the quantity isn't the same, there's ~~———~~ it's almost like AN ELECTRIC CHARGE WITH A KILL. CHEMICALS, HORMONES, SOMETHING, YOU CAN FEEL it in your blood AND TASTE it in the ANIMAL'S blood.

LAST NIGHT it WAS THREE RABBITS, which my BROTHER got ACTUALLY. HE brought them AND offered them to the group AND we totally TORE THEM APART.

MARK WAS— I'VE NEVER SEEN him STRUT, but he WAS PROUD that he WAS the ONE who lANdEd the rAbbits lAst Night. HE WASN'T EXActly doing ANything, I MEAN he didN't sAy ANything, but he WAS just like Not slouching iNto his chAir, ANd kiNd of smiling to himself. ThAt didN't go OVER so well. THE boys put up with it for A little while, ANd theN BAM they WERE All oN top of MARK. But then they WEREN't — he threw them off ANd kNockEd CARl bAck OVER A chAir. Tomas lookEd up ANd growlEd ANd they All stoppEd, but something hAd chANgEd iN thEiR dyNamic, ANd I'm Not sure it's for the bettER.

STRANgE ENERgy toNight. WE'RE goiNg out huNting lATER.

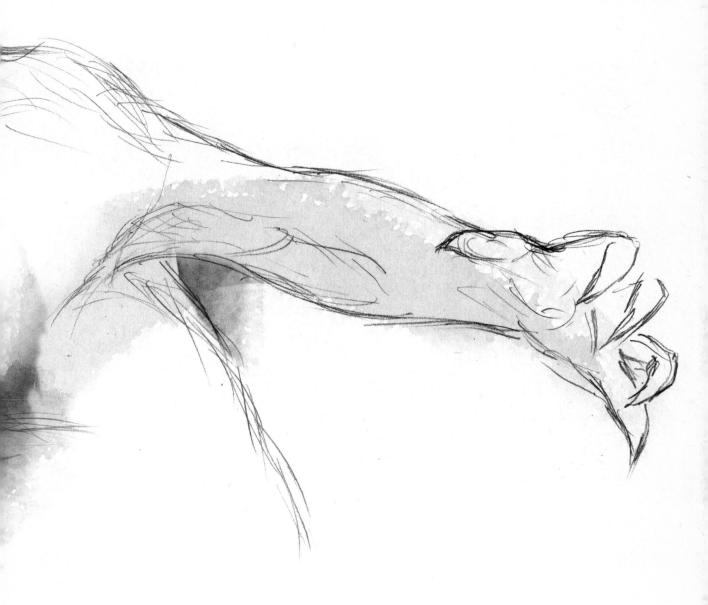

Saturday, May 3rd

Oh god oh god oh god.

There were hunters. We were sleeping in the den and
there were hunters. Tomas was up first and they were focused on him,
I don't know how many there were. We were all wolves.
I remember teeth and claws and silver and blood and tumbling and blood.

I remember two hunters running into the woods and one hunter not running and Mark over him covered in blood and a deep roar from Tomas.

We ran back to the house.
We left the hunter where he was.

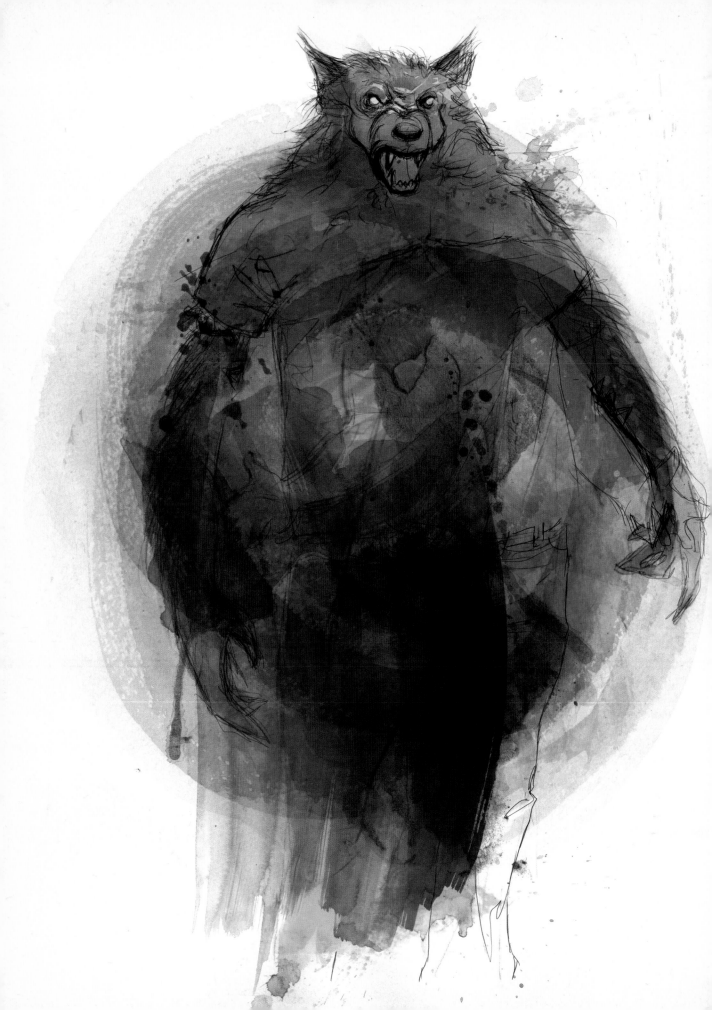

When we got to the house the hunters hadn't found it.
Or found it yet. I don't know. We packed and left. Tomas roared.
YOU DO NOT KILL A HUMAN. HURT THEM. TURN THEM. NEVER
KILL THEM! IT BRINGS THE POLICE!

Mark said he was only trying to protect Tomas, but that was worse.
Danny and Mark both had cuts from the silver weapons.

I DO NOT NEED PROTECTION. I AM PROTECTING YOU!

Tomas hit Mark and Mark flew and he cowered where he landed, but
he was also not cowering at the same time. It may be something
only I'm able to see, but something inside Mark has broken loose
and it's scaring me.

My phone buzzed. A text message from Dave: YOU'VE MADE A MISTAKE.

Monday, May 5th

I'm with Sam. The pack is crashed out at a Motorlodge Inn off the interstate and I was able to slip out and call her. She's been gripping the steering wheel pretty tight. Do you believe me Sam?

"I don't know what to believe. I know you believe it. And you're clearly in some sort of trouble."

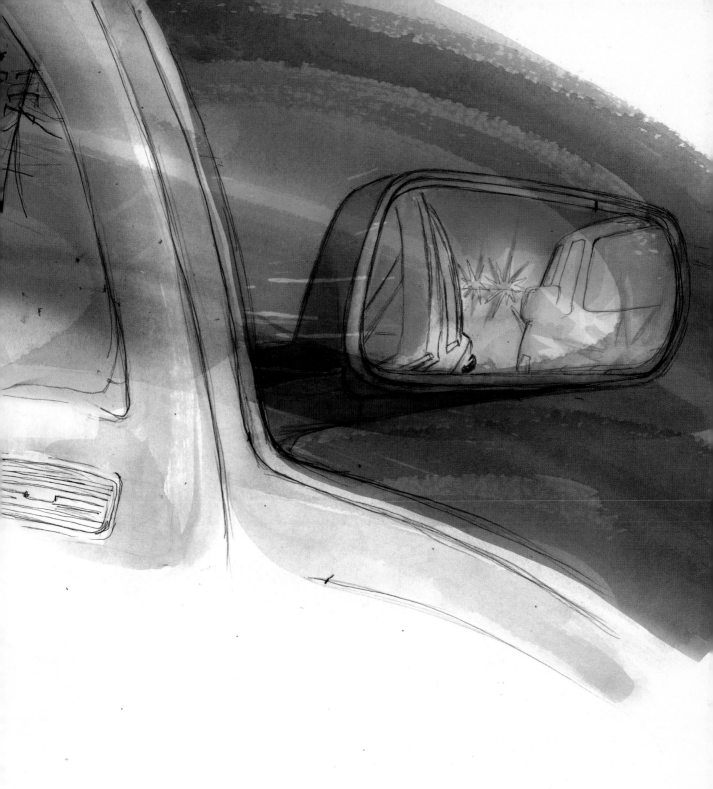

She's worried that, whatever's going on, Mark is still at the Motorlodge. I'm worried too, but we have to do something, and for better or worse that's driving to Case Western and either talking to Marian Bradley or, given that it's after hours, breaking into her lab.

Waiting outside. First waiting for my NERVES to settle down,
but NOW WE'RE waiting for this guy to take one of his EVERY-20-minutes
smoke breaks and wander far enough from the door for me
to get in. Sam wants to know if I want her to go with me. No.

Thursday,
May 8th

~~I can't.~~ I can't. ~~I can't.~~ I can't. I can't.
I have to get it down. I have to write it down.

Inside it was easy enough to find her office. Maybe it goes with
the territory of studying werewolves but she was actually there late.
I can smell her before I get to the lab, and she knows what I am
the minute I walk in.

"I — you're — Hello. I'm Doctor Bradley. You've come to see me."

I say yes, I'm here, I've heard about her work, I want
to know about the "cure", and that I'm —

"Yes, you're only the second lycanthrope I've encountered,
and the first I've conversed with, or been this close to.
Please, would you like to, uh, sit down?"

She says, It's so amazing that you're here, that you're finally
here. I've been waiting for you. Not you but someone like you.
Maybe you. You're here. I'd seen one like you before, but not
so close. CAN I touch — and she touches my arm — you see,
animals and humans already share so much of our DNA, there
are fascinating analogies in human nature and animal behavior,
and here you are, a creature that's literally — when people ask
why I'm researching such foolish science, not even science, bad
movies, it's because they don't understand, they haven't seen a
creature like you, but I have. Why do I do it? It's because I've
been waiting for another one, like you, to come.

She looked  crazy.

I've waited so long and there's so much to learn and I just, I —
will you bite me?

Then Tomas and the pack are here. Tomas says
Your research is a threat to us, Doctor Bradley. Not everyone
dismisses you as a lunatic. Calling attention to our existence, to
those who are paying attention, this endangers us.
Maybe this isn't your intention, but it's the truth.
We need to protect ourselves. If you wish to join us, we
can do this, but we must be careful, and we must take
care of the work you've already done here.

Then ~~XXXXX~~

"I'll bite you," MARK SAYS AND his voice is fake-sweet. HE bears his teeth in A SNARl grin AND he starts shifting AND his bones ARE moving AND EVERYONE'S turning now AND their clothes ARE splitting AND they're growling AND Tomas shouts <u>NO</u> AT MARK AND All of them but it doesn't MAKE ANY difference.

He puts himself between MARK AND the doctor AND EVERYONE is wolves now AND the PACK KEEPS me AWAY AND Tomas AND MARK start tearing AT EACH other.

MARK took Tomas down AND then there were hunters, they were on us.

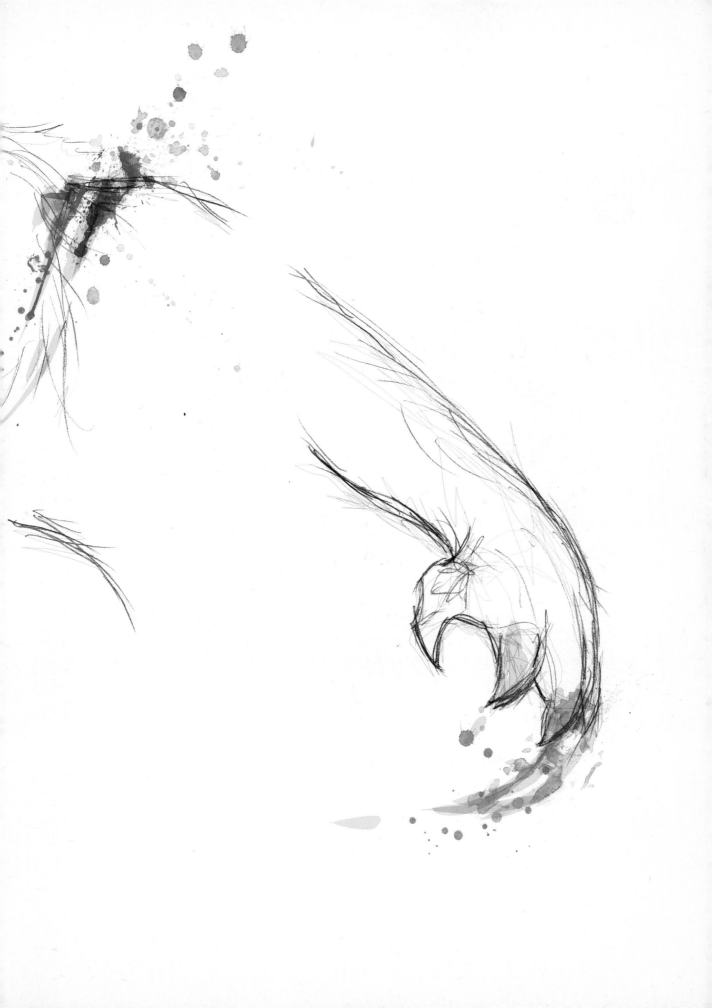

They shot MARK ~~~~~~~~~~~~~~
It ~~~~~ HE WAS TEARING through the room and he
HOWLED and if he wasn't so proud — the Alpha energy — and
after he killed Tomas he was the center of the room and of
course they ~~~~~~~ shot him. The sound of the gun and

the bullet in his chest I could feel it like it was in my chest
like a hammer, it was like a hammer and I fell down and I
was so scared. I wanted to take it all back, just everything
all over again but you can't and I was so scared and I
didn't know how I could help him — MARK PLEASE BELIEVE ME I
love you, I wanted to ~~~~~~~ I saw you there and I saw it, I saw
you turn back into you on the floor and get so small, and I wanted to
help but there was so much blood and I couldn't I just RAN

I don't care what day it is.

~~xxxxxxxx~~ I RAN. That's what I do right? I got to SAM's CAR
AND I ~~xxxxxxx~~ my clothes were kind of shredded — I didn't
turn all the way, I felt like a scream coming up and I wanted
to scream and rip out everyone's throats but whatever in me
froze halfway, I didn't stop myself because I wasn't thinking,
but I couldn't or didn't turn and just ran. When I got to the
car I was me but messed up and I got in and we just drove.

Sam of course is freaking cause look at me, and I'm freaking, sobbing,
and I just say, bad people came and we have to GO NOW, and she's got
no idea, I don't say anything about Mark and we just go. We debate, home?
Not home? And I tell her to drop me at home but down the block and
she does and Mom's still up. I watch her inside at home through the
windows and I stand outside out back in the trees and in the dark
wearing Sam's jacket and I watch and she sets the coffeemaker for
the next day like always and does the dinner dishes and turns off the
kitchen light and goes to bed.

I shiver outside for a while and then sneak
in and pack some of my stuff and go. It can't ~~be~~
be safe for her if I stay there. I couldn't call her because
she'd pick up the phone no matter what time of night, of course
worried sick, and I can't face talking to her yet so
I ~~scribbled out~~ I TEXTED her that Mark had an
accident but that I'm OK and I'm so sorry and I love her and
I'll talk to her soon and I don't ~~scribbled out~~ WHAT IS THIS?
What am I supposed to do? What could I possibly tell her? Or
Sam, or anyone?

I'm not safe with the pack, even if I could find them again. The
hunters will want to take me because of my brother.

THERE'S NO POINT to RECORDING this ANYMORE OTHER THAN I guess it focuses me? Not that it CALMS ME DOWN. So should I calm down now? WHENEVER I'm out in public I don't know who might be wolves or might be hunters — that's not true, I'd totally know by their smell, of wolf or of fear, but I'm afraid to. I DON'T WANT to RECOGNIZE ANYONE this WAY. They'll RECOGNIZE ME.

I CAN'T do this.

I CAN do this but by myself. I don't SEE what choice I HAVE ANYWAY. It's SAFE in the woods. I NEED to get AWAY from here AND live Alone AND TAKE A deer once A month or whATEVER they said AND just fADE into the background, WHERE NO ONE'S going to KNOW whAT I AM, AND I CAN BE whAT I AM.

PUBLISHER'S NOTE

Dr. Marian Bradley, no longer with Case Western Reserve University, denies
that the events described herein took place and points to the lack of any
documentation at the university of the incident, as well as a lack of police
records. A search of Ohio public and private school files reveals numerous
students by the name of Alice who have withdrawn or dropped out; one of
these, Alice Carr, has a brother named Mark who also attended Fairview High
School in Maple Heights. When contacted, the students' mother said simply
that her family's business is her own.

The journal was discovered by a group of hikers in Cuyahoga Valley National
Park, inside a small duffel bag containing articles of clothing and other
personal items.